The Boxcar Children Mysteries

THE BOXCAR CHILDREN
SURPRISE ISLAND
THE YELLOW HOUSE
    MYSTERY
MYSTERY RANCH
MIKE'S MYSTERY
BLUE BAY MYSTERY
THE WOODSHED MYSTERY
THE LIGHTHOUSE
    MYSTERY
MOUNTAIN TOP MYSTERY
SCHOOLHOUSE MYSTERY
CABOOSE MYSTERY
HOUSEBOAT MYSTERY
SNOWBOUND MYSTERY
TREE HOUSE MYSTERY
BICYCLE MYSTERY
MYSTERY IN THE SAND
MYSTERY BEHIND THE
    WALL
BUS STATION MYSTERY
BENNY UNCOVERS A
    MYSTERY
THE HAUNTED CABIN
    MYSTERY
THE DESERTED LIBRARY
    MYSTERY
THE ANIMAL SHELTER
    MYSTERY

THE OLD MOTEL
    MYSTERY
THE MYSTERY OF THE
    HIDDEN PAINTING
THE AMUSEMENT PARK
    MYSTERY
THE MYSTERY OF THE
    MIXED-UP ZOO
THE CAMP-OUT MYSTERY
THE MYSTERY GIRL
THE MYSTERY CRUISE
THE DISAPPEARING
    FRIEND MYSTERY
THE MYSTERY OF THE
    SINGING GHOST
MYSTERY IN THE SNOW
THE PIZZA MYSTERY
THE MYSTERY HORSE
THE MYSTERY AT THE
    DOG SHOW
THE CASTLE MYSTERY
THE MYSTERY OF THE
    LOST VILLAGE
THE MYSTERY ON THE ICE
THE MYSTERY OF THE
    PURPLE POOL

THE MYSTERY OF THE PURPLE POOL

created by
GERTRUDE CHANDLER WARNER

Illustrated by Charles Tang

ALBERT WHITMAN & Company
Morton Grove, Illinois

ISBN 0-8075-5408-1

1 3 5 7 9 10 8 6 4 2

Printed in the U.S.A.

Contents

CHAPTER   **PAGE**

1. A Big Surprise   1
2. Here We Come!   12
3. The Purple Pool   25
4. The Switch   38
5. The Angry Guests   53
6. A Spectacular View   63
7. Stuck!   72
8. Who Did It?   82
9. The Phone Call   94
10. The Letter   103
11. The Mystery Man   115

CHAPTER 1

A Big Surprise

The Alden children were all in the living room of their grandfather's big, comfortable house in Greenfield.

Benny sat on a window seat, gazing out. Rain splattered against the cold glass. Benny sighed. "Isn't it *ever* going to stop? It's been raining for *four* days, and I'm bored."

Henry looked up from the book he was reading and said to his six-year-old brother, "Come on, Benny, we'll play some checkers."

Benny shook his head. "Thanks, Henry,

but I've played a million games of checkers in the last few days."

Henry laughed. "Well, not *quite* a million games. How about if we do that new jigsaw puzzle you have?"

Benny thought for a minute. "I think that puzzle is too easy for a boy who is fourteen like you."

Jessie walked over to them. "Is it too easy for a twelve-year-old girl?"

"I think so," Benny said.

Violet joined them. "How about a ten-year-old girl?"

Benny shrugged. "I think you're all just trying to be nice to me."

"I know!" Jessie said enthusiastically. "Let's ask Mrs. McGregor if we can bake cookies."

"*That* I like," Benny said. "But what will we do after that?"

Grandfather Alden was sitting in a big easy chair in a corner of the room, with Watch dozing at his feet. He folded the newspaper he had been reading and put it in his lap. "You know," he said, "I have to go to New York City tomorrow on business. I'll be there a few days. How would you children like to come with me?"

"To New York?" Jessie cried out, hardly believing what her grandfather had said.

"I've never been there," Benny said.

"None of us has," Violet added.

"Wow!" Henry said. "Would we like to come with you to New York? You bet we would."

Violet ran over to Mr. Alden and threw her arms around him. "Oh, Grandfather, that would be wonderful!"

Mr. Alden rose from his chair. "I'll call the Plymouth Hotel and get rooms for all of you."

He walked into the den and the four children followed him eagerly. He dialed the hotel number and waited for an answer. Then he said, "Reservations, please."

"That's us," Benny whispered to Violet. "We're reser . . . reser . . ."

"Reser*vations*," Jessie filled in.

"That's what I said," Benny answered proudly.

"Sssh," Violet said, as Grandfather continued his conversation.

"This is Mr. James Alden. I have a reservation for a room from tomorrow until Thursday. But now I'm bringing my grandchildren with me. Do you have a suite with three bedrooms and a sitting room?" He looked at the children and smiled. "And perhaps a kitchenette?"

"A *kitchenette*!" Henry and Violet said together.

"You do?" Mr. Alden said. "Good. I'll take that and we'll check in tomorrow afternoon. Thank you." He hung up the phone and went back to the living room with the four children at his heels.

When he had settled in his chair again, he said, "There are some guidebooks to New York City on the second shelf in the bookcase in the den. Why don't you all look through them and decide what you want to do. I'll be working part of the time, so Henry and Jessie, you'll be in charge."

The children found the guidebooks and Violet said, "Let's take them to the boxcar and look at them there."

"It's raining so hard," Benny said.

"We can run down," Jessie said. "A little rain won't hurt you."

"Maybe Mrs. McGregor can give us a snack to take with us," Benny said hopefully.

Jessie laughed. "That sounds familiar, Benny. But it's a good idea."

In the kitchen, Mrs. McGregor was baking an apple pie. "Do you have any cookies and fruit, Mrs. McGregor?" Benny asked.

Mrs. McGregor wiped her floury hands on her apron and opened a big cookie jar on the counter. She took out several chocolate cookies and put them on a plate.

"We're going down to the boxcar. I'll wrap them so they don't get wet," Violet said. She took some paper napkins and put them around the plate. Then she put the plate with the cookies into a big paper bag.

Henry took some pears out of the refrigerator and packed them in the bag with the cookies. "We're ready now, Benny," he said. "Let's go."

The children ran down to the boxcar, which was in the garden. Jessie remembered how they had lived in the boxcar after their parents had died. They had run away because they were supposed to go and live with their grandfather. They had heard he was a mean man. When Mr. Alden found them, they had all realized how wonderful he was. They had happily gone to live with him. Mr. Alden had even brought along the boxcar for the children to play in.

The Aldens climbed into the boxcar and sat on the cushions on the floor. Henry went to the shelf that held the dishes they had found and used when they had lived in the boxcar. He took a plate and put the pears on it.

Benny took a cookie and bit into it. "Very good," he said.

"When didn't you think a chocolate cookie was good?" Henry asked.

"I guess never," Benny replied.

Jessie was already going through a guidebook. Violet and Henry each looked through one, too. "We *have* to go to the Empire State Building," Jessie said.

Benny leaned over her shoulder and looked at the picture. "I know that building." He stooped to look at the caption underneath. "Does that say it's one hundred and two stories high?"

"Yes, Benny! You read that by yourself!" Jessie said.

Benny beamed proudly. He was just learning to read.

Violet was reading about the Statue of Liberty. "We have to take a ferry to get to it. I'll like *that*," she said.

"There's a whole room just of armor at the Metropolitan Museum," Henry said excitedly.

"There's so much to do!" Violet said.

"And don't forget — we have to eat, too," Benny added.

Jessie laughed. "I'm sure there are plenty of restaurants in New York."

The Aldens stayed in the boxcar for a long time, eating their snack and going through

the books. Every few minutes one of them would cry out the name of another thing they wanted to see or do.

At dinner that night, as the Aldens were finishing the delicious chicken Mrs. McGregor had made, Mr. Alden said, "I have some work to do in my office tomorrow morning. If we leave Greenfield in the afternoon, we'll get to New York in time to settle in our rooms and have dinner."

"How long will it take to drive there?" Jessie asked.

"About four hours," Grandfather said. "Now the weather is very cool, so pack warm things. We'll probably go to the theater one night, so you'll want something dressier than jeans for that."

"I'm going to start packing right now," Jessie said.

"Me, too," Violet agreed.

By the time Grandfather was ready to go the next day, the children had been packed and waiting for hours. They started off, waving to Mrs. McGregor, who stood in the driveway with Watch.

"Take care of him," Benny cried out.

"Don't you worry," Mrs. McGregor replied. "We'll do fine."

As Grandfather drove, the Aldens played a variety of games to pass the time. They counted how many blue cars they saw, then red ones. They watched for out-of-state license plates. They played word games.

Finally Mr. Alden said, "We're on the Henry Hudson Parkway, and that's the Hudson River on our right. New Jersey's on the other side of the river."

"Is that the river Henry Hudson sailed on?" Jessie asked.

"Same one," Grandfather said. "Soon you'll see the George Washington Bridge."

After a little while, Benny shouted, "Is that it?" He pointed to a long bridge.

"That's it," Mr. Alden said.

"It's *so* beautiful," Violet said.

"So graceful," Jessie added.

They rode down the highway, admiring

the tall apartment buildings to their right, on the banks of New Jersey, and the lovely park to their left, which Grandfather said was called Riverside Park. Beyond the park were even more skyscrapers. Then they got off the highway and drove to their hotel. All the way the Alden children looked at the big buildings and cars and trucks and crowds of people.

Finally they reached the hotel. Grandfather drove into the garage where a young man in a uniform ran to the car. He opened the trunk with the keys Mr. Alden gave him and piled all the luggage onto a cart.

A garage attendant gave Mr. Alden a ticket. "I'll take care of your car, and the bellboy will take you to the check-in desk."

The family got into an elevator, and soon they were in the hotel lobby.

CHAPTER 2

Here We Come!

"Wow!" Benny said as the Aldens entered the lobby. It was decorated with thick carpeting, large comfortable chairs, and flowered wallpaper. And it was bustling with activity. There were people rushing out the door or into one of the elevators. Guests were checking in and out. Bellhops pushed large carts of luggage across the floor.

The children followed Grandfather to the reservations desk. "Hello, I'm James Alden," Grandfather said to the young woman behind the counter. "I've reserved a suite of rooms for the next few days."

"Welcome to the Plymouth," the woman said, smiling. She pushed some buttons on the computer in front of her and looked at the screen. "Hmmm . . ." she said after a moment. "I see your name here, but someone's cancelled your reservation."

"That's odd," Grandfather said. "*I* certainly didn't cancel it."

"I wonder how this happened," the woman said. "Well, Mr. Alden, I'll see what we have available."

"What seems to be the problem?" asked a man behind the counter. He had a friendly face and a mop of red hair.

"Mr. Parker, it seems that Mr. Alden's reservation was cancelled by mistake," the woman said.

"I'll handle this," said Mr. Parker with a sigh. Then, turning to Grandfather, he said, "I'm the assistant manager, Don Parker. I'm very sorry about this mix-up. I'm sure I can find rooms for you." He looked at the computer. "Ah, here's a lovely suite on the fifth floor," he said. "With a view of the park."

"That sounds perfect," Grandfather said.

Just then an attractive woman with light brown hair came out of an office on the left. "James Henry Alden!" she exclaimed, walking over to greet Grandfather. "It's been a long time since your last visit!"

"It certainly has, Ms. Ames," Grandfather said with a hearty smile. "It's good to see you again. I didn't know if you were still working here."

"Sure am! And I've been promoted to manager," Joan Ames explained. "I see you've met my assistant manager, Don Parker."

"Yes, he was just helping us out of a little mix-up," Grandfather said.

"Really?" Ms. Ames asked. "What?"

"Oh, it's nothing to worry about," Don Parker said with a pleasant smile. "I've taken care of it."

"Let me introduce my grandchildren. This is Henry, Jessie, Violet, and Benny." Mr. Alden motioned to each of them in turn. "Ms. Ames takes good care of me whenever

I'm in town," he explained to the children.

"Your grandfather is one of our favorite guests," Joan Ames told them. "I'm so glad that he brought all of you with him this time."

"We've never been to New York City before," Jessie said.

"Well, then, you've got a lot of things to see here," Ms. Ames replied.

"Do you think we'll find a mystery?" asked Benny. "We're good at solving mysteries."

"I'm afraid there are no mysteries here!" Don Parker said with a chuckle.

"Well, I've got to run, but if you need anything at all during your stay, please let me or Mr. Parker know," Ms. Ames said.

"Thank you," Grandfather said, as the manager turned and headed back to her office.

Grandfather filled out the check-in forms while the children looked around the bustling lobby, their eyes wide.

"Look at that man over there!" Violet whispered suddenly.

A man had just gotten off the elevator. He

had silvery hair and a long pointed nose. He was wearing dark sunglasses, a hat pushed low over his face, and a tightly belted raincoat. He kept his head down and walked quickly across the lobby and out the front door as if he didn't want to be seen.

"He certainly looked mysterious," Henry said.

"I knew it," Benny said happily. "A mystery to solve!"

The Alden children laughed.

When Grandfather had finished checking in, he turned to his grandchildren. "We can go up to our room now. A bellhop will bring up our luggage for us."

"I'm sorry, Mr. Alden," Don Parker said, his face flushed. "I can't seem to locate the bellhops. They may be taking breaks. But if you'd like to leave your luggage, I'll make sure someone brings it up to your room immediately."

"That's okay. We can carry our things," Henry offered.

The children picked up their small suitcases, and Grandfather took his suitcase and garment bag. As they started toward the elevator, they could hear Mr. Parker muttering under his breath, "I wish Joan would have a word with those bellhops . . ."

Grandfather led the way to the elevator. After all the Aldens and their luggage were inside, he pushed a button marked "5." "We're in room 502," he said.

"Look," Benny said to Violet, pointing to the ceiling. "There's a mirror up there!"

Violet looked up and waved at Benny in the mirror. Benny grinned and made a funny face back at her.

When the elevator reached the fifth floor, the doors opened to reveal a long, red-carpeted hallway.

"Rooms 500 to 510 are this way," Benny said, reading the sign on the wall and pointing to the left.

"You read that very well," Jessie told Benny.

The first door had number 510 on it. "It looks like we're all the way at the end," Grandfather said.

Midway down the hall, a man in a gray

suit was talking to a hotel maid. Next to her was a large cart filled with cleaning supplies and fluffy towels. As they approached, the Aldens couldn't help overhearing the couple's conversation. "Why wasn't my room made up?" the man was asking angrily.

"But it *was* made up," the maid answered. "I did it this afternoon, just as I always do."

"No, you didn't," the man replied. "Look — it's a mess."

As the man pushed the door to his room wide open, the children caught a glimpse inside. Sure enough, it *was* a mess. The two double beds were both unmade, the sheets and blankets lying in heaps on the floor. The wastebasket was overflowing. There were crumpled towels on the dresser.

"It's even messier than when I left this morning," the man said angrily.

"That's odd," the maid said. She had a strange look on her face. "I'll fix it up right away," she assured the man, hurrying inside. "I'm very sorry!"

Down the hall, a door was open, and a dark-haired woman was poking her head out.

She was obviously paying close attention to what was going on.

"Who's she, I wonder," Jessie whispered.

"She looks like a spy!" Violet whispered back.

The woman heard the children whispering, and saw that they were looking at her. Giving them an angry glare, she quickly pulled her door shut, slamming it behind her.

"Well," Henry said. "What was that all about?"

Before anyone could answer, Benny ran to the end of the hall, and found the door to their suite. "502!" he called out.

The suite was just as beautiful as they'd hoped. It was bright and sunny, with large windows facing Central Park, the large, beautiful park in the center of the city. There was a small sitting area with a couch and two chairs grouped around a low table. To one side was a small kitchenette with a tiny refrigerator, stove, and sink. Off the sitting room were three bedrooms: a large one with a king-sized bed for Grandfather, and two smaller rooms, each with a pair of double beds for the children.

The Aldens stood at the windows, looking out at the view. The hotel was on a busy street, with cars rushing by and people hurrying down the sidewalks. Central Park spread out before them, filled with trees, whose branches were bare. Tall buildings surrounded the park. Along the side of the park was a line of old-fashioned horse-drawn carriages.

"Look! Horses!" cried Violet, who loved animals of all kinds.

"Would you like to go for a carriage ride later?" Grandfather asked.

"Yes!" the children shouted together.

"Let's unpack, and I'll make some reservations," Grandfather suggested. "Afterwards we'll take our ride through the park."

The children eagerly went to unpack their bags. Henry and Benny took one bedroom, and Jessie and Violet took the other. "Wow!" Benny said, bouncing up and down on his large bed, "this bed is much bigger than my bed back home!"

Meanwhile, Violet was putting her toothbrush and toothpaste on the counter in the bathroom.

"Oh, how wonderful!" she said, carrying a little basket of toiletries out of the bathroom. "Look at all these goodies." Jessie and Violet poked through the basket, taking out each tiny bottle of shampoo and lotion and bar of soap. Each one was wrapped in pretty yellow paper with a label that said THE PLYMOUTH HOTEL.

"Look what I found!" Benny cried, walking into the girls' room with a chocolate bar in his hand. "There's a little refrigerator in the kitchen, and it's filled with chocolates, and nuts, and juice, and soda — "

"You're not going to eat that before dinner, are you?" asked Grandfather, who had poked his head into the room. "I've made a reservation at one of my favorite restaurants."

"Then let's go!" said Benny, putting the chocolate bar down.

As the Aldens were leaving, they met a couple with a boy about Benny's age standing outside room 501, next door. The man had a garment bag and a large suitcase in one hand, and with his other hand he was digging in his pocket for the room key.

"May I help you?" Grandfather asked.

"No, but thank you," the man said, finding the key at last. "They couldn't find a bellhop, so we had to carry all our things up ourselves."

"Well, it looks like we're going to be neighbors," Grandfather said, putting out his hand. "James Alden."

"Edward Grant. Pleased to meet you," Mr. Grant responded, shaking Grandfather's hand. Then he introduced his wife, Laura, and his son, Bobby. Mr. Alden introduced his grandchildren.

"We've just come in from Massachusetts. Where are you all from?" Grandfather asked.

"Chicago," said Mrs. Grant. "But we used to live here. We thought it would be fun to come back and visit the Big Apple."

"I wish I had a big apple right now. I'm *hungry*!" Benny chimed in, and everyone laughed.

" 'The Big Apple' is a nickname for New York City, Benny," Grandfather explained.

"Well, we were just on our way to dinner, and I guess we'd better get going. I wouldn't want my grandson to starve. Nice meeting you."

"Enjoy your dinner," Mr. Grant said.

"See you later," Violet called out, as they headed down the hallway.

When they got to the elevator, Jessie turned to her grandfather. "We had to carry our own luggage, too. Isn't it strange that they still haven't found any bellhops?"

"Yes, it is," Grandfather said. "This used to be a really first-class hotel. That sort of thing would never have happened."

"Do you think something is wrong?" Jessie asked.

"Like what?" Henry said.

Jessie answered, "I don't know. But where are all the bellhops, and why was our reservation cancelled?"

"I told you there would be a mystery," Benny said.

Grandfather laughed. "I'm sure *nothing* is wrong. You children are *always* looking for mysteries."

CHAPTER 3

The Purple Pool

The Aldens ate in a fancy restaurant that had long white tablecloths, candlesticks on every table, and music playing softly.

Afterwards they went to the line of horse-drawn carriages for a ride. The children were surprised to see that, like the horses, which were different shades of brown, gray, and black, the carriages were each a little different, too. And so were the drivers. Some had on elegant top hats and tails, and others had clownish, colorful clothes.

The Aldens picked out a white carriage with a heart-shaped window in the back. The driver, a pretty young woman, told them funny stories about the city and pointed out the sights as they rode through the park. The bright lights, and all the activity in the city, even though it was nighttime, excited the Aldens. They listened carefully to everything the driver said.

The next morning, the children woke up bright and early, eager to explore all the places they'd read about in their guidebooks. Even Jessie, who liked to sleep late, was ready to get going.

"I have some phone calls to make before breakfast," Grandfather said. "But maybe you children would like to try out the swimming pool on the roof."

"A swimming pool on the *roof*?" Benny asked.

"There's a glass-enclosed deck up there," Grandfather explained. "And the pool's heated, so it's nice and warm."

"Great idea, Grandfather," Henry said.

"We'll meet in the coffee shop for breakfast at nine o'clock. That will give you enough time for your swim," Mr. Alden suggested.

The children put on their bathing suits, with T-shirts and shorts over them. The hallway was silent, and it seemed that no one else was awake yet.

But when they reached the top floor, they were startled to see that someone else *was* awake. Waiting at the elevator doors was the same mysterious man they'd seen in the lobby when they'd arrived. He was wearing a blue terrycloth robe and the same dark sunglasses he'd had on the day before. His silvery hair was wet.

"Hello!" Benny said as the children got off the elevator. "Did you just go for a swim? How was — "

Before Benny could finish his question, the man pushed past the Aldens into the elevator. It was as if he hadn't even seen or heard them. The children stared as the doors closed behind him.

"What a *strange* man," Jessie commented.

"He's not very friendly," said Benny.

"Maybe he's just shy," suggested Violet, who was a little shy herself.

"I don't think so," Henry said. "Just like yesterday, he seemed to be in a big hurry to get somewhere."

"It's almost as if he doesn't want anyone to see him. Maybe he's got something to hide," Jessie said.

"Come on!" Benny called, impatient to go swimming. He ran ahead toward the big, frosted-glass doors with the word POOL painted on them.

In front of the doors, a young man was seated at a desk. He had blond hair and was wearing a white T-shirt that said THE PLYM- OUTH HOTEL on it. On the desk was a clip- board and a pile of fluffy white towels.

"Hi. Here to swim?" the man asked.

"Absolutely!" cried Benny.

"Great. My name's Mike. I'm in charge of the pool. I just need you to sign in." He handed the clipboard to Henry, who noticed that there was one other name on the sign- in sheet — *Mr. John Smith*. He figured that must be the mysterious man. Henry wrote down his name, and then handed the clipboard to the others.

When they'd all signed in, Mike glanced at the signatures. "So," he said, pointing to Violet. "You must be . . . Benny?"

"No, that's me!" Benny said.

"Oh! Then you must be . . . Henry?" he asked Violet.

She giggled. "No, I'm Violet."

"I'm Henry," said Henry.

"Then this must be . . . Jessie." Mike turned toward Jessie. "Is that short for Jessica?"

To the surprise of her sister and brothers, Jessie just smiled and looked down, not saying a word. Usually it was Violet who was shy, and Jessie who was friendly and outgoing. When Jessie looked up, the children could see that her cheeks were red.

Mike smiled. "Let me give you a quick tour. In here is our exercise room." He motioned through a doorway on their right to a large room filled with all kinds of equipment: stationary bicycles, rowing machines, and weights. "There are locker rooms if you need to change into your suits — "

"Nope! We've already got ours on," Benny said.

"Well, I can see Benny is ready to hit the pool," Mike said. "Take a towel, and go right ahead."

Benny eagerly grabbed a towel and pushed through the doors to the pool. The others were about to follow him, when suddenly he burst back through the doors. "Wow! *Wait* till you see this!" he cried.

"Yeah, I bet you've never seen a pool on top of a building before," Mike said.

"And I've never seen one with purple water!" said Benny.

"*Purple* water?" Mike said, smiling. "I see you like to kid around, Benny."

"I'm not kidding!" Benny replied.

Mike looked at Benny curiously, then pushed open the door to the pool and looked in. "*What?*" they heard him say, and then he quickly disappeared inside. The Aldens ran after him.

The pool room had windows on three sides. Even the ceiling was made of glass, and the sunlight streamed in. There were rows of deck chairs, and on one side there was a small round whirlpool with steaming hot water. In the center of the room was a large rectangular swimming pool — filled with bright *purple* water!

Mike was kneeling at the edge of the pool. "*What* is going on?" he was saying to himself.

"The water isn't supposed to be purple, is it?" Henry asked.

"No — it's *definitely* not," Mike said. "I can't imagine what's happened."

"Look," Jessie said, picking up an empty box that was underneath one of the deck chairs. "Purple dye," she said, reading the label. She handed the box to Mike. "Why would anyone want the water in the pool to be purple?"

"That's *exactly* what I'd like to know," Mike said. "Listen, I'd better call the manager. If you kids want to, you can use the whirlpool over there. It's not purple, too, is it?"

"No, it looks fine," said Henry. "Is there anything we can do to help?"

"No, thanks," Mike answered. "I'll take care of it. But I'm glad you found this box of dye, Jessie. Who knows, it might be an important clue." He smiled at her as he left the pool room.

Again, Jessie blushed, and gazed after Mike.

The Aldens slipped out of their T-shirts and shorts, and placed them with their towels on a deck chair next to the whirlpool. Benny was the first to dip his foot in the water. "Gosh!" he said, pulling it out quickly. "This is really hot!"

"Yes," Henry said. "It's not for swimming. It's just for relaxing."

One by one, the Aldens stepped cautiously into the steaming water and sat down on the ledge around the whirlpool. The water was shooting out of little jets in the sides of the pool, swirling and bubbling all around them.

"I think Jessie has a crush on Mike . . ." Henry teased, after a moment.

Jessie's face, which was already flushed from the steaming water, turned even redder. "Oh, Henry, I do *not*," she said. "He's just . . . nice, that's all."

"I think he's very cute," Violet said.

"Anyway, we've got more important things to talk about," said Jessie, quickly changing the subject. "Like who would dye a swimming pool purple?"

"If I didn't know better, I'd think it was Violet," Henry said with a smile. "After all, purple *is* your favorite color, isn't it?" he asked his sister.

"Yes, but not for a swimming pool!" Violet said, grinning.

"What about that mysterious man? He was up here before us," Jessie said. "He might have dumped the dye in."

"He did seem in an awful hurry to leave," Henry pointed out.

Just then, Mike and Don Parker burst through the doors. "Oh, my goodness!" Mr. Parker said when he saw the pool. "It really *is* purple! How could this have happened?"

The children couldn't hear everything the two men were saying, but they saw Mike showing Mr. Parker the empty box of dye that Jessie had found.

"I'm getting too hot," Benny complained. "Isn't it time for breakfast?"

"It's almost nine o'clock. Let's go meet Grandfather in the coffee shop," Jessie suggested.

The Aldens dried off and gathered up their clothes. Walking past Mr. Parker, they overheard him telling Mike, "We'll just have to drain the pool, clean it, and refill it. But I'm going to find out who did this, and why. I'll get to the bottom of this."

The children went to their rooms to change, and then took the elevator down to the lobby. Grandfather was standing in front of the coffee shop, chatting with a dark-haired woman.

"Look, Jessie," Violet whispered, grabbing her sister's arm. "That's the same woman we saw last night, peeking out of her door."

"Yes, it is," Jessie agreed.

"These are my grandchildren," Grandfather said. "This is Karen Walsh. Her room is a few doors down the hall from ours."

Karen wasn't any friendlier than she'd

seemed the night before. "Yes, I saw you all coming in last night, and I was a bit worried. Children can be *so* noisy sometimes."

"We're not," said Henry, a bit offended by her remark.

"My grandchildren are very grown-up," said Mr. Alden, but Karen looked unconvinced. She stood with her arms crossed and her lips pressed tightly together. "How was your swim?" Grandfather asked the children.

"You were up at the pool this morning?" Karen said. Suddenly she seemed very interested in the Aldens. "How was the water?"

"It was purple!" Benny blurted out.

"*Purple?*" Grandfather repeated.

"What do you mean?" Karen asked.

"The water was bright purple," Henry explained. "Someone had dyed it."

"Why?" Grandfather asked.

"No one knows," Benny replied.

"They're going to drain the pool and clean it out," Violet explained.

"Do they know who did it?" Karen asked.

"No, but we did find an empty box of dye," Jessie said. "Mike thought that was an important clue." She blushed slightly.

"Who's Mike?" Grandfather asked.

"Oh — he's just the pool attendant," Jessie said, blushing a deeper shade of red.

"You found a box of *dye*?" Karen said. "What are they going to do about it?"

"We heard Mr. Parker say he'd get to the bottom of it," Benny offered.

"He did? Excuse me, I'm afraid I have to run," Karen said.

"Aren't you going to have breakfast?" Grandfather asked.

"Oh, yes, well . . . I'm not very hungry after all. There's something I must take care of first," Karen said, and she hurried back to the elevator.

"What an odd woman," Henry said.

"Yes, it seems like there are a *lot* of strange people here," Jessie said, "and one of them put purple dye in the pool. The question is, *who*?"

"And why?" added Henry.

CHAPTER 4

The Switch

"Aren't we going to eat breakfast?" Benny asked. "I'm hungry!"

"Well, that's no surprise," Henry said with a laugh.

"Let's go on in," Grandfather said, leading the way into the coffee shop. The hostess brought the Aldens to a large round table in the center of the room and gave each of them a menu.

"*Everything* looks good!" Jessie said as she read the list of delicious breakfast specials.

When the waitress came and took their

orders she said, "I'm Jane. I'll be as fast as I can."

But the wait for their food seemed endless. Each time Jane came from the kitchen with a tray of food, Benny said, "Is *that* ours?"

At last, Jane came to their table, carrying an extra-large tray loaded with food.

"Benny, your blueberry pancakes look delicious," Grandfather said. He stirred sugar into his steaming cup of coffee.

"I'll give you a taste if you'd like, Grandfather," Benny said, pouring a thick stream of syrup over the top of his stack of blue-flecked pancakes. "Want some syrup, Jessie?" he asked.

"No, thanks. I'm going to put sugar on my waffles and fruit," Jessie said.

Violet had already started eating her cereal. "What's wrong?" Grandfather asked when he noticed the strange look on her face.

"This tastes *awful*," Violet said.

"Is the milk sour?" Grandfather asked.

"No," Violet said, "it's not that. The cereal tastes funny . . . sort of salty."

"Yuck!" Jessie said after taking a big bite

of waffle. "My waffle tastes salty, too!"

"My pancakes are great!" Benny said, munching happily.

"How about you, Henry. How are your scrambled eggs?" Grandfather asked.

Henry took a bite of his eggs and made a face. "My eggs taste sweet!"

"I wonder . . ." Jessie said thoughtfully. "Hand me the salt and sugar, please." Henry passed them to her, and Jessie sprinkled a little from the saltshaker onto a finger. She took a taste. "This tastes *sweet*." Then she spooned out a little from the sugar bowl and took a taste of that. "*Salty!*" she cried. "The salt and sugar are mixed up!"

"That's why all of our food tastes funny!" Henry said.

"Not mine," Benny said. He had already eaten half of his pancakes. "Mine tastes good! I'm glad I only used syrup!"

"I'll speak to Jane and see if we can get this straightened out," Grandfather said. But try as he might, he couldn't get her attention. Suddenly, it seemed as if everyone in the coffee shop needed something, and all the

waiters and waitresses were running from table to table.

"Yes, I'll get you a fresh omelette," the Aldens heard Jane saying to one table. "Certainly I can bring you another bowl of oatmeal," she said to another. "I just can't understand what's happening this morning," she muttered to herself.

At last she came to the Aldens' table. "I believe the salt and sugar have gotten mixed up," Grandfather told her.

"What?" the weary-looking waitress said.

"We noticed that all our food tasted funny," Jessie explained, "and so I checked the salt and sugar. They've been switched."

"Really! How did that happen?" Jane said. "I'll bring you a new order right away. But I wonder . . ." She paused.

"What are you wondering?" Henry asked.

"Well, *everyone's* had some kind of complaint this morning about their food," she explained.

"Not me!" said Benny, gobbling up the last bite of his pancakes.

Jane smiled at Benny. "I wonder if the salt

and sugar were switched at other tables, too." She walked over to the table next to the Aldens'. "Could I borrow your salt and sugar?" she asked.

"Sure," the man sitting there said gruffly. "I'm not eating another thing until you bring me some fresh coffee. This tastes terrible! I keep putting more sugar in it, and it just gets worse."

"Right away, sir," she said. But first she did the same test Jessie had done earlier. "The salt and sugar on this table were mixed up, too," she said after tasting each one. "I'm so sorry. I'll bring you some fresh breakfast immediately."

"Thank you," Grandfather said. The Aldens watched as Jane motioned to the other waitresses and waiters. They stood talking in a corner for a moment, and then all of them disappeared into the kitchen. After a few minutes they came out carrying empty trays, and went from table to table, removing the saltshakers and sugar bowls.

People were beginning to grow impatient. They complained loudly as they waited for fresh food to replace their salty cereal and sugary eggs. A number of guests got up, angrily muttering about "being too busy to wait."

"It's a good thing my meeting isn't until eleven o'clock this morning," Grandfather said. "I've got plenty of time to wait. But some people don't."

"Some people are *very* angry," Violet said.

"Look, there's Karen Walsh," Benny said. "I thought she said she wasn't hungry."

Karen Walsh was sitting at a table in the corner. Strangely enough, she seemed to be the only person in the restaurant, besides the Aldens, who looked calm. She was watching all the action with a small smile on her face. There was no food on her table, just a cup of coffee and a notebook, in which she was writing.

A few moments later Don Parker came in, looking very worried. His red hair was a mess, and his shirt and tie were rumpled. It seemed that some of the guests had complained angrily at the front desk. Mr. Parker spoke briefly to the hostess of the coffee shop, and then went from table to table, apologizing and encouraging everyone to be patient. Their breakfasts would be served as soon as possible.

The Aldens overheard one angry woman say, "Are you the manager of this hotel?"

"Well, I'm the assistant manager," Mr. Parker explained. "I couldn't find the manager anywhere. But don't worry, we'll give you all a free breakfast to make up for this inconvenience."

"Won't it be expensive for the restaurant to give everyone a free breakfast?" Henry asked Mr. Alden.

"Yes, it will," Grandfather said. "But when you run a hotel, it's important to keep your guests happy."

"Isn't that the manager's job?" Violet asked.

"I wonder where Ms. Ames is," Jessie said.

At last Jane brought food for all the Aldens except Benny. While they were eating, he began to grow restless. "I think I'll go say hello to Karen Walsh." Benny headed to her table. She was still writing in her notebook, but when Benny came over she slammed the notebook shut and began stuffing it into the large leather bag on the seat beside her. She didn't look at all happy to see Benny.

"Hello," Benny said.

"What do you want?" Karen asked.

"I just thought I'd come say hi, but if you're busy — " Benny started.

"Yes, I am," Karen said. "I've no time to talk. I have work to do."

Benny returned to the Aldens' table. "She's *still* not very friendly," he said glumly. "She said she was working."

"What kind of work?" Jessie asked.

"I don't know — she was writing in that notebook, and she definitely didn't want me to see it," Benny said. "She hid it away as soon as I got there."

"What could she be writing that's such a secret?" Violet asked.

They watched as Jane approached Karen's table to refill her coffee cup. Again, Karen hid the notebook in her bag.

"I've been wondering about the salt and

sugar mix-up," Jessie said, changing the subject. "At first I thought it was just an accident. But it looks like they were switched at
every table."

"Then it couldn't have been an accident,"
Henry said.

"Why would anyone want to do that?" Violet asked. "I mean, it would take a long time,
so you'd have to have a really good reason."

"It must have taken a long time to dye the
pool purple, too," Jessie pointed out.

"I think it's a mystery!" Benny said excitedly. "It's a good thing we're here to solve
it!"

After breakfast, Grandfather left for his
meeting, and the children decided to take a
walk and see some of the nearby sights.
Henry carried the map, and Jessie carried
the guidebook, and they all stayed close
together on the crowded sidewalks. They
walked down Fifth Avenue, amazed at how
much there was to look at. Everywhere they
turned, there were big buildings, store windows filled with all sorts of things arranged

in imaginative displays, and crowds of people walking quickly, dressed in different kinds of clothes.

On one corner, the Aldens stopped to watch two men and a woman singing in perfect harmony. There was a hat on the ground in front of them, and some people walking by stopped to listen and then threw a few coins in the hat.

The Aldens reached St. Patrick's Cathedral. It was the biggest church they'd ever seen. It filled an entire city block, and its tall spires reached up toward the sky. The children walked up the steps and went inside, where it was quiet and peaceful compared to the noise and bustle outside. There were long aisles with rows and rows of pews, and beautiful stained-glass windows.

After leaving St. Patrick's, the children crossed the street. "Look at that!" cried Benny, running over to a huge bronze statue. It was a man struggling to hold a giant globe on his shoulders.

"That's Atlas," Henry explained. "He was a character in Greek mythology who held the whole world on his shoulders. That's where the word *atlas* — you know, a book of maps — comes from."

"According to our guidebook," Jessie said, "this area is called Rockefeller Center."

The Aldens walked to a large ice-skating rink set below street level. The rink was surrounded by flagpoles with flags from many different countries flapping in the breeze.

"Wow," said Violet as the children stood above the rink, looking down at the skaters. On the opposite side of the rink was a large golden statue of Prometheus, another character from Greek mythology, that shone brightly in the sun.

Jessie looked in the guidebook and said, "The book says that at Christmastime they have a huge tree here, over sixty feet tall and covered with lights."

The children stood watching the skaters. There was a woman in a short pink skirt who was doing jumps and turns in the middle of the ice. "She's wonderful," Jessie said. "I wish I could skate like that."

A bunch of teenaged boys skated rapidly

around the ice. There were some couples holding hands, and a young girl who couldn't take a step without falling down.

"I wish we had brought our skates," Violet said.

"I bet we could rent some," Henry pointed out. "Let's go see."

There was a place to rent skates, and the children put them on and headed out to the ice. They whizzed around and around to the music.

Jessie was a very good skater, always eager to learn something new. Shyly, she approached the woman in the pink skirt and asked if she would mind showing her how to do some of the turns and jumps. The woman smiled and said, "I'd love to. Just watch me." In no time, Jessie was able to perform a new jump.

After a little while, the children began to get tired, and of course Benny was hungry. They returned the skates, and Jessie said, "Isn't it wonderful? That woman taught me a new jump. And I thought New Yorkers were supposed to be unfriendly."

"I guess that's just not true," said Henry.

It was lunchtime now, and the sidewalks were filled with people leaving their offices and going out to eat or shop. As the Aldens approached their hotel, they found themselves walking in front of a couple who were talking very loudly. Although they didn't mean to eavesdrop, the Aldens couldn't help overhearing what the couple were saying.

"Lucille," the man said, "I know you're very angry that The Plymouth fired me, and I am, too. But don't worry, I'm handling it. I've already started to do some things — "

"The Plymouth?" Violet said. "That's our hotel." She peeked over her shoulder and saw a pretty woman with chin-length dark hair and a man who looked like her but was a little older. Violet quickly nudged her sister. "It's a maid from our hotel," she whispered. "The one we saw in our hallway last night."

"*What* are you doing about it, Malcolm?" Lucille demanded.

"I said I was taking care of it," Malcolm said. "Calm down."

"They should *never* have fired you," Lucille insisted. "And I don't care what *you* have in mind — I'm doing something about it myself."

"Don't, Lucille. I know how *you* handle things. Just be careful," Malcolm said. "Don't you get fired, too."

By now the Aldens were very curious. They strained to hear what Lucille and Malcolm were saying. But at the next corner, the couple turned and disappeared into the crowd.

"They certainly sounded angry," Violet said.

"I wonder what he meant when he said he was taking care of it," Jessie said.

"And I wonder what *she* meant by 'I'm doing something about it,' " Henry said.

"What do you think she'd do that might get her fired?" Violet asked.

Jessie said, "This hotel is getting more and more mysterious."

"That's just the way I like it!" said Benny.

CHAPTER 5

The Angry Guests

"Where are we going to eat?" Benny asked.

"Good question," Henry replied.

"I know," Violet said. "Let's buy some food and fix lunch in our kitchenette."

"That would be fun," Jessie agreed.

Benny was doubtful. "Where are we going to buy food? I haven't seen a grocery store anywhere."

"He's right," Jessie said.

"There must be some place around here," Violet said.

The Aldens walked a few blocks and then Benny exclaimed, "Look! Over there!"

"It's a deli," Henry said.

"That's food," Benny pointed out.

The children ran into the delicatessen and bought ham, cheese, bread, fruit, cookies, and hot chocolate mix.

When the Aldens got back to The Plymouth with their bag of food, Jessie looked around the lobby, her eyes wide. "There are an awful lot of people here," she said.

Henry laughed. "It's New York City, Jessie. There *are* 'an awful lot of people here.' "

"It seems more than usual," Jessie said, thoughtfully.

Benny grabbed Jessie's hand. "Come on! Let's go upstairs and eat. Never mind the people."

"Benny's right, as usual," Henry said.

They went up to their rooms. They took dishes out of a little cupboard in the kitchenette and made ham-and-cheese sandwiches. They put the sandwiches and fruit on plates. Henry put water up to boil on the tiny stove. When it was bubbling, he put the hot chocolate mix into four cups and poured the water over it. Benny carefully stirred the mixture and licked the spoon.

They took their plates over to a table next to a window and ate contentedly.

"We forgot mustard," Benny said.

"We'll just have to rough it," Jessie said, smiling.

They all laughed and finished their lunch.

"What are we going to do this afternoon?" Benny asked.

"Before *we* do anything," Jessie said, "I know what *I* want to do."

"What?" Violet asked.

"I don't care what you said, Henry. I think there were a *lot* of people in the lobby. I want to see why," Jessie said.

"Let's go," Benny said. "It's another mystery."

"We'll go," Henry answered, "but I'll bet there's no mystery."

In the lobby, there was a crowd of people around Joan Ames, all calling out different things.

"There are no towels in my bathroom."

"The hangers are gone from my closet, and all my clothes are on the bed."

"I have no shower curtain."

"My pillows have disappeared."

"You see!" Jessie said. "I was right!"

Ms. Ames, looking very upset, said in a firm voice, "Please calm down! Everything will be taken care of."

"I'm *never* coming to this hotel again," an angry man said.

"Me, either," said someone else.

Suddenly Don Parker came running over. "What's happening, Joan? Can I help you?"

"You can certainly help our guests," she answered.

She called out, "Please! This is Mr. Parker, our assistant manager. He will take care of each one of you. Just tell him your problem."

Joan whispered to Mr. Parker, "I'm going to try to find out how this happened." Then she ran off.

"Don't worry — I'll take care of every-thing," he called after her.

"Do you suppose we could help Mr.

Parker?" Violet asked her sister and brothers.

"I don't know how," Henry answered.

"We can ask him," Benny said.

"Right! Let's go!" Jessie added.

The Aldens ran over to Mr. Parker, who was surrounded by guests. "Can we help in any way?" Jessie asked him.

Mr. Parker sighed. "I wish Ms. Ames had stayed here." Then he said, "I guess you could just tell the guests I'll talk to each one personally and take care of their problems."

The children circulated around the lobby and spoke to each guest who was upset. When things were quieter Jessie said, "I think we should go back to our rooms and try to figure out *what* is going on here."

"I said right away there was a mystery," Benny said, proudly.

Back in the suite, Henry got some paper and a pencil. "I'll write down everything that's been strange since we got here."

Jessie began, "Well, first of all our reservation had been cancelled. And there were no bellhops."

"And then, before we went into our

rooms, a man was complaining to the maid, Lucille. He said she hadn't cleaned his room. But *she* said she had," Violet noted.

"And then, that Karen Walsh poked her head out of her door and listened," Benny added.

"And the pool was dyed purple," Jessie said.

"And you liked Mike," Violet said, grinning.

"I *didn't*, and that is *not* part of the mystery," Jessie replied.

"You forgot the man who always wears sunglasses," Henry said.

"Right! And the salt and sugar were mixed up in the coffee shop," Violet went on.

"And Karen Walsh didn't want me to see what she was writing," Benny said.

"And we heard Lucille and Malcolm arguing on the street," Jessie said.

Henry said, "Go slower. I can't write that fast."

"And last," Violet said, "all those people in the lobby complaining that things were missing from their rooms."

"What does it all mean?" Benny asked.

The Aldens were all quiet. "I don't have *any* idea," Jessie said.

"I don't either," Henry and Violet said together.

"This is a *really* mysterious mystery," Benny said.

Just then there was a knock on the door. Benny ran and opened it. Mr. Grant, from next door, and his son, Bobby, were standing there. "I'm sorry to bother you," Mr. Grant said. "But I wonder if I could use your phone?"

"Of couse," Jessie said. "Is yours out of order?"

"It's *gone*," Bobby said.

"Gone?" Violet asked.

Mr. Grant shrugged. "Do you believe it? Someone took our phone! I want to call the desk and tell them."

The children exchanged glances. Just then Mr. Alden came into the room. As Mr. Grant called the desk, the Aldens started telling their grandfather everything that had happened.

They all talked at once, until Grandfather held up his hand. "Wait a minute. One at a time."

The children took turns until they had told Mr. Alden everything.

"Wow!" Bobby said.

Mr. Alden said, "Well, it all does *seem* strange, but I'm sure it can be explained."

"Grandfather," Benny said, sounding disappointed, "don't you think it's a *real* mystery?"

Mr. Alden laughed. "Well, maybe, Benny, but I think the hotel has to solve it. I'll talk to Ms. Ames, if it will make you children happier."

"Do, Grandfather!" Jessie said.

"Meanwhile," Grandfather said, "you children are here to enjoy yourselves. What do you have planned for tomorrow?"

"How about the Empire State Building?" Jessie asked.

The others all agreed. Benny said to Mr. Alden, "Can Bobby come, too?"

"I think he has to ask his father," Mr. Alden replied.

"Can I, Dad? Can I?" Bobby asked eagerly.

"Well, I guess it would be all right. How old are you, Henry?" Mr. Grant asked.

"Fourteen," Henry replied, standing up tall.

"I guess you can look after Bobby," Mr. Grant said. "Meanwhile, Bobby, we have to leave the Aldens to themselves."

As they left, Benny called out to Bobby, "See you tomorrow!"

CHAPTER 6

A Spectacular View

The next day, the Aldens decided to avoid the coffee shop. Instead, they ordered breakfast from room service. Jessie called downstairs and placed their order. Soon a waiter wheeled in a table with their food.

After enjoying juice, milk, and a basketful of warm cranberry and banana muffins and sweet rolls, they were ready to go. Grandfather told the children which bus would take them to the Empire State Building and which bus would bring them back to the hotel.

"I'll meet you here around dinnertime," Grandfather said, "and you can tell me everything you saw."

The Aldens stopped at the Grants' room to pick up Bobby.

"Ready?" Henry asked.

"Yes, I am!" cried Bobby.

"All last night he kept talking about how excited he was to be going to the Empire State Building," said Mr. Grant.

"Me, too!" cried Benny.

"Have fun!" Mrs. Grant called as the childen left.

The bus stop was just a block from the hotel, and the children didn't have to wait long before a bus arrived. Grandfather had given them tokens, and they each slipped their tokens into the fare box as they got on the bus. There were three seats together in the middle of the bus, so Benny, Bobby, and Violet sat down, and Jessie and Henry stood, holding on to the metal rail over their heads.

When they reached Thirty-fourth Street, Henry rang the bell, and the bus stopped right in front of the Empire State Building. They got off the bus and then stood on the sidewalk, staring up at one of the tallest and most famous buildings in the world. Standing right below it, they couldn't even see the top.

"I thought a lot of the buildings here in New York were tall," Benny said, his eyes wide. "But this one is *really* tall."

"Sure is," Bobby said. "I can't wait to get to the top!"

"Let's go!" said Benny eagerly.

The older children smiled at the two excited boys. Henry led the way inside.

The lobby was quite large, and the walls and floor were covered with marble. There were lots of elevators and shops, and at first the Aldens weren't sure which way to go.

" 'To the Ob . . . observ . . .' " Benny tried to sound out the sign on the wall, but it was too difficult.

"Good try," said Jessie. " 'To the Observation Deck'."

A short line of people curved back from a ticket booth, and the children went to wait at the end.

The line moved quickly. After they had bought their tickets and picked up some pamphlets with information, the children followed the people ahead of them to an elevator.

Soon they were shooting up to the top of the building. The elevator went so quickly that the lighted sign over the door counted off the floors they passed by tens: 10, 20, 30, 40, 50 . . .

"Hey!" Benny said. "My ears are popping like they do in an airplane."

"That's because we're going up so high so quickly," Jessie explained.

60, 70, 80 . . .

At last the elevator doors opened, and they were on the 86th floor. Benny and Bobby were the first out onto the observation deck, which ran all the way around the building.

"This is great!" Benny said. It was a clear, sunny day, and they could see for miles in every direction. The city lay spread out before them: rows of small buildings looked like toys, and tiny buses and cars moved along the streets. People were so small, the children could hardly see them.

"We're facing north," Jessie said. "See, there's Central Park. I think I can see our hotel."

"What's that building over there?" Benny asked, pointing to a tall, beautiful building.

"That's the Chrysler building," Henry said, checking his pamphlet.

Off to the west, the children could see the Hudson River, alongside which they had driven into New York, with New Jersey stretching out on the other side. On the east they could see another river, the East River, with several bridges stretching across it.

"That's Brooklyn over there," Jessie said. "And look! There's a plane taking off at the airport!" Beyond Brooklyn they could see the ocean.

To the south, they could see the tip of the island of Manhattan and lots of skyscrapers in an area Henry said was called Wall Street. "Those two really tall buildings are the World Trade Center — the Twin Towers. They're even taller than the Empire State Building."

"Wow!" Benny said. He could hardly believe it.

Jessie pointed out the Statue of Liberty, in the harbor beyond the Twin Towers. It looked very tiny.

The children walked around the observation deck, looking out at the city from all sides. There were even telescopes that you could look through for a quarter, and each of the children took a quick peek.

When they had seen all they wanted to, the children went inside and took another elevator up to the very top — the 102nd floor. Emerging from the elevator, they found themselves in a tiny room. There was no outside deck here, but they peered out the windows at the city below, now even tinier.

When they returned to the 86th floor, Benny said, "May we get a souvenir?"

"Sure," said Jessie. The Aldens selected a small model of the Empire State Building and a postcard to send to Mrs. McGregor. Bobby bought a pencil sharpener and eraser shaped like the tall, pointed building.

"Should we take a bus back?" Jessie asked when they were back down in the lobby.

"Let's walk for a little while and look around," Violet suggested. "When we get tired, we can get on the bus."

"Good idea," Henry said.

"What about if we get hungry?" Bobby asked.

"I think you and Benny are going to be good friends," Jessie said with a laugh.

"I'm hungry already," said Benny.

"How about a hot dog?" Henry suggested. "There's a vendor on the corner."

The man selling hot dogs was wearing a bright blue apron. He stood behind a metal cart topped by a blue-and-yellow striped umbrella. His cart held a steaming pile of large, soft pretzels covered with salt. There was also a pan of roasted chestnuts, which the man stirred with a long spoon, turning over the nuts as they browned. Hot dogs were cooking on a small barbecue. Bobby and Benny decided to share a hot dog with lots of mustard and ketchup. Henry got a hot pretzel with mustard, and Jessie and Violet

each had a packet of roasted chestnuts. They walked as they ate, enjoying their snacks.

"Be careful not to drip mustard on your clothes," Henry told Benny and Bobby. But the boys were having too much fun eating and talking to listen.

CHAPTER 7

Stuck!

Back at the hotel, Jessie suggested that they go for a swim.

"You want to see Mike, don't you?" Henry teased.

"*No,*" Jessie insisted. "I just thought it might be fun."

"I wonder if the pool has been cleaned yet," Violet said.

"There's only one way to find out," said Benny.

"Yeah, let's go see!" Ever since Bobby had heard about the purple pool up on the roof, he couldn't wait to see it for himself.

In the elevator, Jessie pushed P for pool. The doors closed, and the children felt the elevator start to rise.

"Look," Benny said to Bobby, pointing up to the mirror on the ceiling. He made a funny face at Bobby, who made a funny face back. The two boys were laughing when suddenly the elevator stopped. It sat perfectly still for several seconds, but the doors didn't open.

The children looked at each other, curiously. Two lights were lit up on the dial over the door — 8 and 9.

"What's happening?" Violet asked nervously.

"It looks like we've stopped between the eighth and ninth floors," Henry said. "I'm sure we'll be moving again in no time."

"Yes," Jessie said, trying to sound more sure than she felt. "This probably happens a lot in elevators."

"I live in a really tall building in Chicago," Bobby said. "And once the elevator just got stuck."

"Got *stuck?*" Benny echoed, his eyes wide.

"What do you mean, 'got stuck'?" Violet asked in a small voice.

The silence in the elevator was beginning to make them all feel a little uncomfortable.

"I don't really know for sure," Bobby said slowly. "I think something had gone wrong with the way the elevator works."

"What happened?" asked Jessie. She was trying to stay calm so the others wouldn't be scared.

"The people in the elevator called the superintendent, and he fixed it," Bobby explained.

"But we don't have a telephone," Benny said, his voice trembling a little.

"Sure we do," Bobby said with a reassuring smile. He walked over to a small door built into the panel of buttons. Bobby opened it and pulled out a telephone that had been hidden inside. "It's for emergencies," he explained. "The elevator at home is just like this, and my parents showed me how to call for help."

"I'm glad you're here!" Benny said, looking very relieved.

"We all are," said Jessie.

"Hello, this is Bobby Grant, and I'm stuck in the elevator," Bobby said into the phone. "Which elevator? I don't know . . . oh, okay. I'll check." Bobby turned to the Aldens. "Do you see a number anywhere?"

"There it is," Jessie said, pointing over the door. "Elevator number three."

Bobby told the person on the other end, then he hung up the phone. "That was Mr. Parker. He said not to worry, they'd fix it as quickly as they could."

"Who's worried?" asked Benny. He felt much happier now that he knew someone was going to help them.

"I just hope it doesn't take too long," Violet said.

"Why don't we play a game to keep busy?" Henry offered.

Jessie smiled at her brother. "Good idea."

"What kind of game can we play in an elevator?" asked Benny, doubtfully.

"Well, how about Twenty Questions," suggested Jessie.

"Hooray! My favorite!" cried Bobby.

"I forget how to play," Benny said.

"Let's all sit down on the floor, and I'll explain," Jessie said. The children sat in a small circle with their legs crossed. Jessie leaned back against the wall of the elevator. "Each one of us takes a turn. Let's say it's my turn first," she began. "I'll think of a person, a place, or a thing."

"Like the president," offered Violet.

"Or the moon," said Henry.

"Or a peanut butter sandwich!" Bobby said. Even after the hot dog, he was still hungry.

"Yes," Henry said. "Or a peanut butter sandwich."

Violet went on, "We have to guess who or what it is by asking questions. If it takes us more than twenty questions to figure it out . . ."

"Then I win!" said Jessie.

"I remember now," Benny said.

"I'll go first." Jessie thought for a moment and then smiled, "Okay, I'm ready — it's a person. Violet, why don't you ask the first question?"

Violet was looking around the elevator nervously, her face pale. Her sister knew that thinking of a question would be a good distraction.

"Let's see," Violet said, "Is it a real person or make believe?"

"Real," said Jessie.

"I'll go next," cried Benny. "Boy or girl?"

"Boy," Jessie said.

Henry took the next turn. "Have we ever met him?"

Jessie burst out laughing. "Yes, you've definitely met him!"

Now all the children were concentrating on the game and had forgotten they were sitting on the floor in an elevator. "Why don't you ask a question, Bobby?" suggested Jessie.

After thinking for a moment, Bobby asked, "Is he young or old?"

"Young," said Jessie.

"Tall or short?" Benny asked.

"Short," said Jessie. "But medium for his age."

"Is he thin or fat?" Violet asked.

"Medium," said Jessie, and then she couldn't resist adding, "but he loves to eat."

Henry laughed. "Is he stuck in this elevator with us?"

"Why, yes," replied Jessie, beginning to giggle.

"Is it Benny?" Henry asked.

Before Jessie could respond, Benny said, "Wait a minute, it's my turn!" Then he thought for a brief moment and grinned. "Is it me?"

"Yes, it is," said Jessie, smiling broadly. The children all laughed. A second later they heard a noise, and finally the elevator began to move.

"Hooray!" Violet cheered.

The elevator went back down to the lobby. When the doors opened, the children were surprised to see that a crowd had gathered. The people clapped their hands as the Aldens and Bobby got off. Benny smiled and bowed deeply.

Mr. Parker pushed his way to the front of the group. "Are you children all right?" he asked. "Someone switched off that elevator, although I can't imagine why. I'm glad you knew how to use the emergency phone."

"We wouldn't have, if it hadn't been for Bobby," Henry said. "He saved the day." Bobby beamed proudly.

"So what was wrong with the elevator?" Violet asked.

"As it turns out, *nothing*," Don Parker said. "It took me a little while to find someone in our maintenance department, but when he checked, he said someone had just switched off the power for that elevator. I hope you weren't nervous being in there so long."

"So long?" Benny said. "It didn't seem like very long."

"We were having a good time playing a game," Jessie explained.

"Is the elevator still broken?" a man in the crowd asked.

"No, it wasn't broken, just turned off temporarily," Mr. Parker explained. "It's fine now."

"What do you mean *someone* turned it off?" Henry asked.

"Just what I said," Don Parker answered. "I don't know who did it, or why. But I'm going to find out." With that, he turned and walked away.

"Sounds like another piece of the mystery," Violet said.

"It sure does," Jessie agreed. "I think it's about time we figured out what's going on here."

"Let's go back to our suite," Henry suggested.

"I think I might take the stairs," Violet said quietly.

"Violet," Jessie said gently but firmly to her sister, "Mr. Parker said the elevator was fixed. And you know what they say: When you fall off a horse — "

"I know, you get right back on," Violet said quietly. "I guess you're right." She followed the others back into the elevator. And this time, it worked fine. In a few seconds, they were on the fifth floor.

CHAPTER 8

Who Did It?

The Aldens dropped Bobby off at his room. He couldn't wait to tell his parents all about his trip to the Empire State Building — and the adventure in the elevator, too.

After waving good-bye to his new friend, Benny turned to his brother and sisters. "So, are we still going to the pool?"

"Sure," said Henry. "Why don't we have lunch first, and then we'll go up to the pool."

The children had put the leftovers from the day before in the refrigerator, and there was enough for lunch. When they had finished eating, they went up to the roof deck, dressed in T-shirts and shorts with their bathing suits underneath.

"Hello!" called Mike as the Aldens approached his desk.

"We're here to swim!" called Benny. "What color is the pool today?"

"I'm sorry. You can't swim in it just yet. We had to drain it and scrub it, and it hasn't been refilled. But maybe you'd like to try out our exercise room," Mike suggested.

"That sounds like fun," said Violet.

In the exercise room, there was something for everyone.

Henry went over to look at the rack of loose weights. Selecting one small barbell for each hand, he began curling his arms up and down.

Meanwhile, Benny had wandered over to a machine that had a sort of television screen on it. "What's this?" he asked.

"That's a rowing machine," Mike said. "I'll be over there to help you in a second. Let me just get your sisters started."

Jessie and Violet had gotten on the exercise bicycles.

"Do you girls like to ride?" Mike asked.

"Yes," said Jessie quietly. Being around Mike seemed to make her nervous.

"We go all over Greenfield on our bicycles," Violet added. "I wish we could have brought them with us — but I'd be scared to ride my bicycle around New York City."

"A lot of people do it," Mike said. "But it can be pretty dangerous with all the cars. You'll like these bikes — you don't have to worry about traffic." Mike grinned. "And you can make it easier or harder to pedal just by pushing this button, depending on how hard a workout you want. First, you have to start pedaling."

Jessie began pedaling, and Mike pushed a button on the panel at the front of her bike. "There, try that," Mike said. "That's like riding on flat ground."

Jessie pedaled very fast.

"Too easy?" he asked. He pushed another button. "How about hilly countryside?"

Jessie pedaled harder.

"Still too easy?" Mike pushed another button. "This is mountain terrain."

By now Jessie was getting out of breath. "Okay, okay!" she said, laughing. "How do you stop this thing?"

Mike laughed, too, and pushed another button. "Better?" he asked.

"Yes," Jessie said. Now she was pedaling at a slow, easy pace, as if she were riding along the roads of Greenfield. "Thank you."

"Glad to help you," Mike said with a smile, adjusting Violet's bike to the same level.

As he walked away, Violet turned to her older sister. "I think he likes you," she whispered with a big smile.

Jessie looked straight ahead, as if she was concentrating on pedaling. But Violet thought she could see a small smile tugging at the corners of her sister's mouth, and she was sure her cheeks weren't pink just from riding.

Meanwhile, Mike was helping Benny with the rowing machine. "Sit in the little seat," he told Benny. The seat was on the ground, facing what looked like a TV screen. Mike strapped Benny's feet securely into place, so that his legs were bent up in front of him. Then Mike showed Benny how to "row" by pulling a small bar toward him while pushing back with his legs.

"This is hard to pull," Benny said.

Mike pushed some buttons on the side of the machine. "There, that ought to be easier."

As Benny pushed with his legs, the seat slid backward. When he had pushed the seat nearly all the way back, his legs were straight out in front of him. Then he bent his legs and let the tension on the bar pull him forward again.

"Now pull on the bar and push back with your legs again," Mike explained. "Back and forth. You can watch the little boat moving across the screen to see how fast you're going."

"Neat!" cried Benny. "But this is hard work!"

"That's the point," Mike said, smiling.

After he had gotten each of them going on

their exercises, Mike headed back out to the front desk. "Yell if you need anything," he called over his shoulder.

When Mike was gone, Henry turned to his sisters and brother. "We've got to solve this mystery," he said, panting slightly as he lifted a barbell to his chest and brought it back down.

"We can add the broken elevator to the list of strange things that have happened here," Jessie remarked.

"I can't believe how many things have gone wrong or gotten mixed up!" Violet said.

"They could be accidents, couldn't they? Maybe this is just a bad hotel," Benny said.

"Grandfather wouldn't stay here if it weren't a good hotel," Violet pointed out. "And anyway, most of the things that have happened *couldn't* have been accidents. Remember the purple pool?"

"And the sugar and salt mix-up?" added Jessie.

"Yeah, you're right," Benny admitted. "But why would someone do all those things?"

"Could someone not like this hotel?" Jessie asked. "And want it to close down?"

"But who? And why?" asked Benny.

Jessie shrugged. "I don't know."

"That's what makes it a mystery," Henry said.

"Who are our suspects?" asked Jessie.

"There's Lucille, the maid," Henry said. "Remember how angry she was that the hotel had fired Malcolm? She said she was doing something about it, and he warned her not to get fired. She'd certainly be fired for dyeing the pool purple and turning off the elevator switch. Maybe this is what they were talking about."

"And she knows her way around the hotel. In her uniform, she could get into lots of places other people couldn't," Jessie added.

"Remember when we first got here?" Benny asked, pushing back and forth. "The man down the hall complained to her about his room not being cleaned up? She said she was sorry, but maybe she wasn't. Maybe she didn't clean it on purpose!"

"You know who else was listening to that

conversation?" Violet asked. "Karen Walsh. She always seems to be around when there are problems."

"Karen was in the coffee shop during the salt and sugar mix-up, too," Jessie recalled. "She was one of the only people who didn't seem bothered. It was almost as if she expected it."

"When I went over to talk to her that morning, she was afraid I'd see what she was writing in her notebook," Benny reminded them. He had grown tired and had stopped rowing. "I thought that was pretty mysterious."

"And she was very curious to hear about the purple pool. A little *too* curious, I thought," Jessie said.

"But why would *she* want to hurt the hotel?" Benny asked.

"Maybe she works for another hotel that's trying to put this one out of business," Henry suggested, putting his weights back on the rack.

"I just thought of another suspect," Jessie said. "Remember we saw one person up here, besides Mike, the day the pool was dyed?"

"That mysterious man!" said Benny. "I'll bet you anything it's him. He always looks as if he's just done something wrong and doesn't want anyone to catch him."

"And I saw his name on the pool sign-in sheet," Henry remembered. "John Smith. Doesn't that sound like a made-up name?"

"Sure does," Violet agreed. She had gotten off her bike and gone to get a drink at the water fountain near the door.

"So we've got some suspects. Now what? We have no *proof* that any of them did anything wrong," said Jessie.

The children all sat quietly thinking, tired from their exercising.

"I think we should follow each one of them," Benny said. "That's what a real detective would do. Maybe then we'll get some proof!"

"I like that idea, Benny," said Jessie. "Let's do it!"

"Shhhh!" said Violet, who was still standing near the door. In a loud whisper she said, "Look who's out there talking to Mike!"

The Aldens crowded around their sister, trying to see. It was Karen Walsh, carrying her notebook as always.

"Are you *sure* I'll be able to use the pool tomorrow?" Karen was asking Mike.

"Yes, ma'am. We're working as quickly as we can," he answered.

"And how do you know someone won't dye it orange tomorrow?" Karen asked.

"*Orange?*" Mike said. "Well, I certainly hope that won't happen — "

"Yes, I'll bet you do," Karen said. "But you can't be sure, can you?" And with that, she turned on her heel, and headed for the elevator.

"This is our chance!" Benny whispered. "We should follow her!"

"What about the other suspects?" Violet asked.

"Violet, you come with me," said Jessie, grabbing her sister's arm. "Benny and Henry, you two try to find out more about Lucille and the myserious man."

Violet and Jessie waited until Karen had gotten on the elevator and the doors had shut behind her. Then they hurried out and looked up at the panel over the elevator, which showed what floor the elevator was on. It stopped when it got to nine.

"What's she doing on the ninth floor?" Violet asked. "Her room's on the fifth floor, like ours."

"I don't know, but we're about to find out," said Jessie. "Come on!" Jessie headed for the door to the stairs. "We'll walk down. Waiting for the elevator will take too long."

"Hey, girls, how'd you like the exercise bikes?" Mike called out just then.

"They were fun," Jessie said, turning around to talk to him.

"Sorry we have to run, but we're on an important mission," Violet explained. "Come on, Jessie."

"Well, have fun!" Mike said with a grin.

CHAPTER 9

The Phone Call

Reluctantly waving good-bye to Mike, Jessie followed Violet down the stairs to the ninth floor. When they got there, they looked around for Karen, but she was nowhere to be seen.

"Rats!" Jessie said to her sister. "We've lost her."

The only person they saw was a maid with a cart full of cleaning supplies and fresh towels. She smiled at the girls as she left room 907 and entered room 908.

"Look." Violet pointed. "There's a door

opening." The door was halfway down the hall. Someone peered out and then left the room hurriedly. It was Karen. Violet pulled her sister behind the maid's cart where they couldn't be seen.

"I wonder whose room she's coming out of," Jessie said.

"I don't know." Violet poked her head out to look. "But she's writing in that notebook again. Uh-oh! Now she's coming this way! Duck!"

Just then, the maid came out of room 908. "I always forget something," she was muttering to herself. Leaving the door to room 908 open, she disappeared down the stairs.

Karen had been watching the maid. From behind the cart, Violet and Jessie saw her look around, as if to make sure no one was watching her. Then she ducked into room 908.

"What's she *doing* in there?" Jessie whispered.

The two girls scurried across the hallway as quietly as possible, and flattened themselves against the wall. Violet, who was closer to the open door, peeked into room 908.

"What's she doing?" Jessie asked.

"She's looking in the closet," Violet reported. She watched Karen sliding the closet door open and shut.

"Now what's she doing?" Jessie asked. It was frustrating not being able to see for herself.

"She's looking at the bed — and *under* the bed," Violet said.

The door to the stairs opened, and Benny poked his head out. Jessie saw him just in time and put a finger to her lips, motioning to him to keep quiet.

"We're looking for Lucille," he whispered.

"She's not here," Jessie said. "Now go away before Karen Walsh comes out and sees you!"

Benny ducked back into the stairwell.

"What's she doing?" Jessie prodded her sister.

"She's going into the bathroom. I wonder what she's looking for."

"I'll go check the room she was in before."

Jessie darted down the hallway. She discovered that the room Karen had emerged from didn't have a number like all the other rooms. Instead, there was a sign on the door which read SUPPLIES. What had Karen been doing in the supply closet?

When Jessie got back to room 908, Violet quickly pulled her behind the cart. "She's leaving the room now! Don't let her see you."

Again, the girls were well-hidden behind the cart, and Karen didn't see them. She walked down the hall and got on the elevator.

"What was she doing in there?" Jessie asked, coming out from behind the cart.

"Just poking around — maybe looking for something," Violet said. "I don't think she took anything out with her, though."

"Maybe not this time," Jessie said. "But she still might be the one who took all those things from people's rooms."

"Do you think she's the guilty one?" Violet asked her sister.

"We still can't say for sure," Jessie said. "Maybe Henry and Benny have discovered something more definite."

*   *   *

Henry and Benny weren't having any more luck than their sisters. They had walked down the stairs, too, stopping on each floor to see if they could find Lucille. At last, they located her on the third floor. She was carrying a stack of fresh towels into one of the rooms.

The two boys watched Lucille for several minutes, hoping to see her do something that might be a clue. But nothing she did looked at all out of the ordinary. She went from one room to the next, vacuuming the floors, making the beds, dusting the furniture, and replacing the used towels with clean ones.

"Come on, let's go," Benny said at last. "This is boring."

"It sure is," said Henry. "And we haven't discovered anything to help us solve the mystery."

But just then, something *did* happen.

Lucille had just come out of the last room in the hallway. She looked quickly from side to side, as if she sensed that she was being watched. Then she went back into the room.

"Look!" Henry said. "I think she's up to something."

They saw her sit down on the bed and pick up the phone.

"Who do you think she's calling?" Benny asked.

"I don't know," Henry said. "We'll have to listen."

"That's not polite," Benny said.

"I think in this case it's all right," Henry said.

Outside the open door, they could hear Lucille's voice, even though she was obviously trying to keep it low.

"Malcolm, I'm going ahead with my plan," she said, sounding tense. "I can't help it; I'm still angry. I think it's worth a try. Don't worry — I know what I'm doing. I just wish it didn't make me so nervous."

Henry and Benny looked at each other, their eyes wide. It certainly sounded like Lucille might be the culprit.

"After I've done it, I'll tell you what happened and what their reaction was," Lucille said. "How about if we meet in the lobby

tomorrow after my morning shift?"

They could tell she was about to hang up, so the boys hurried back down the hallway and up the stairs to their room.

"Wait until Violet and Jessie hear about this!" Benny said.

The children met in the suite to compare notes on their suspects. First they made four cups of hot chocolate. Then, sitting on the beds and sipping from the steaming mugs, the girls told how suspicious Karen's behavior had been. But no one could decide what it meant.

"What till you hear what *we* heard," Benny said. Then he and Henry repeated Lucille's phone conversation.

"It certainly sounds like she's plotting something for tonight or tomorrow. We'll have to keep an eye out," Jessie agreed.

"Do you think we should tell someone?" Violet asked.

All the children thought for a moment.

"No," Henry said at last. "We don't have any real, hard evidence, and anyway, all of the other pranks have been harmless. I'm sure Lucille — or whoever is doing this — isn't going to hurt anyone."

"I just hope she doesn't stop the elevator again," Violet said. "Especially with us in it!"

Grandfather came back shortly after that, and the Aldens had dinner at a wonderful restaurant in Chinatown. The children were amazed to see that all the signs in the neighborhood were in Chinese and the telephone booths were decorated to look like little pagodas.

"I feel like I'm in another country!" Benny said, wide-eyed.

"Welcome to the big city!" Grandfather said with a chuckle.

When they returned to the hotel that night, it seemed that everything was calm, and there had been no more pranks. But the Aldens all wondered what the next day would bring.

CHAPTER 10

The Letter

The next morning after break-
fast, the children sat in the lobby. They
hoped they'd see Lucille and Malcolm and
maybe find out what was going on.

While they waited, they enjoyed themselves just watching the people going in and
out.

"I'll never get over all the different kinds
of people in this hotel," Violet said.

"Me, too," Benny agreed. "Look, there's
Mr. Parker. He's sure in a big hurry." Benny
pointed to Don Parker, who was rushing to-

ward the elevators carrying a pile of papers.

Just then some pieces of paper fell from the pile in Don Parker's hands and drifted to the floor.

The Aldens ran after him. "Mr. Parker, wait!" Jessie called out.

Benny bent down and picked up the papers. "Wait, Mr. Parker," he shouted, too. But Don Parker was already in the elevator and didn't hear them. As Violet ran toward him, the doors closed and the elevator started its trip up.

"What should we do with these papers?" Benny asked.

"We don't know what floor Mr. Parker is going to, and there were a lot of people in the elevator, so I guess we should take the papers to his office," Henry said.

As usual, Benny practiced his reading. He looked down at the papers in his hand and read slowly, out loud, "Our plan is work . . . working. Soon I'll be . . . running the hotel . . ."

At the same time, Violet, Jessie, and Henry all said, "*What?*"

"Did I read it wrong?" Benny asked with concern.

Violet said firmly. "We really shouldn't be reading Mr. Parker's papers. It isn't right."

Jessie said, "Let's go sit in that corner and talk about this."

The children went to a quiet part of the lobby and sat down on some leather chairs. Henry said slowly, "I think what Benny read is very suspicious."

"I agree," Jessie said, "and I think, since so many strange things have been happening here, we have a right to read the rest of what's on that paper."

"We do?" Benny asked.

Jessie took the papers from Benny's hands and looked at them. "Benny was reading from a letter," she said. "It's written on the hotel letterhead. And this is what it says:

Dear Nancy:
Things are going very well. Our plan is work-ing. Soon I'll be running the hotel. Then we can get married as we have wanted. Just as we decided, I have done many things to make Joan Ames look

*as if she can't manage a big hotel like The Ply-
mouth. I've messed up guests' rooms; switched the
sugar and salt; pulled a switch to stop the elevators;
and many other things. My favorite was dyeing
the pool purple — my favorite color! All in all,
it makes Ms. Ames look like she isn't doing her
job. You know what that means. The owners will
fire her, and I'll get her job.*

"There's more," Jessie said, "but I've read
the most important part."

"I can't believe it!" Violet said. "Mr.
Parker was doing all that deliberately, to get
Ms. Ames fired."

"He really is a mean man," Benny said.

"What should we do?" Violet asked.

Henry said, "Well, Grandfather is probably still in the coffee shop having his second
cup of coffee. I think we should take the letter
to him. He'll know what to do."

The Aldens all walked to the coffee shop
and looked around. When they saw Grandfather, they hurried to his table. He looked
surprised to see them. "I thought you were
going to sit in the lobby."

"We were, Grandfather, but we found something you should see," Violet said.

Jessie handed him Don Parker's letter. Mr. Alden looked at it. "But this is something Mr. Parker wrote. How did you children get it?"

"He dropped it in the lobby," Benny said. "We ran after him but he went up in the elevator before we could stop him. Then I started reading it, just to practice and . . ." Benny stopped, out of breath.

"Grandfather, please read the letter," Henry said. "It's important."

Mr. Alden read silently and then looked at his grandchildren. "I can't believe it," he said.

"Neither could we," Jessie said, "but Mr. Parker *did* write it."

Mr. Alden sighed. "I think we have to take this to Ms. Ames right away."

In her office, Joan Ames read the letter carefully. Then she put it down and shook her head. "It's Don's handwriting. No doubt about it. I have to admit, I suspected that he was up to something, but I didn't want to believe it. He always seemed so pleased when it looked as if I had made a mistake."

Just then Mr. Parker walked into his own office, which was right next to Joan's. As he went by, she called out "Don, would you come in here for a minute?"

"Yes?" he asked, coming in.

Joan stood up and said sadly, "Of course, you know that a lot of things have been going wrong here."

"That's been quite obvious," Mr. Parker answered.

"Well," Joan Ames said, "there are going to have to be some changes in management."

A smile appeared on Don Parker's face and he quickly erased it. "Yes?" he said again.

In a strong voice Joan Ames said, "Don, you're *fired*."

"Me?" he shouted. "*Me? Why me?*"

"Because of *this*," Ms. Ames said, showing him the letter.

Don Parker's face paled. "I . . . I . . . didn't write that," he stuttered.

"Don," Joan Ames said, "It's your handwriting. It's written in the purple pen that you always use. And earlier this morning I went into your office to get some envelopes, and I saw the phone that belonged in room 501. I wondered about it then. Why would you have a guest's phone in your office?"

"That's the Grants' phone!" said Benny.

Don Parker saw that he had been beaten. "All right, I did do all those things. I wanted your job. I can do it better than you do it. I know it. I deserve it."

At that moment, Lucille walked into the office, looking nervous but determined. "I have to talk to you and Mr. Parker," she said to Ms. Ames.

"What's she doing here?" Benny whispered.

"Can it wait?" Joan Ames asked gently.

"No . . . please . . . it's about my brother, Malcolm," Lucille began. "He worked very closely with Mr. Parker. Mr. Parker fired him last week for no reason at all. Malcolm was wonderful at his job, and there had never been any complaints about him. I think you should rehire him."

Ms. Ames turned to Mr. Parker. "Why *did* you fire him, Don? You told me he wasn't efficient."

"I might as well tell you the truth, since I'm leaving anyway," Mr. Parker said. "Malcolm *was* good at his job — too good — and too smart. I was afraid that he would figure out what I was doing. So I fired him."

Don Parker looked around the room. Then he looked at the Aldens. "You kids are too smart for your own good. Well, I guess there's nothing else to say. So long, Joan," he said, and left.

Ms. Ames smiled at Lucille. "Of course, I'll hire your brother back. In fact, I happen to have an opening for an assistant manager."

Lucille smile happily. "Oh, thank you, Ms. Ames, so much."

Violet said shyly. "Can I ask you a question, Lucille?"

"Of course," Lucille answered.

"The other day we were walking in front of you and your brother on the street, and we heard you talking. We weren't eavesdropping. We couldn't help overhearing. You both were talking about 'taking care of' something and 'going to do something about it myself.' It sounded so mysterious."

"And then yesterday we heard you saying you had a plan that made you nervous," Benny piped up.

Lucille laughed. "The plan was to come in to see Ms. Ames and discuss Malcolm's problem with her. I was nervous because I didn't know what she'd say."

The children laughed, and so did Joan Ames and Grandfather. "That certainly explains everything," said Mr. Alden.

"Well," Ms. Ames said, "you Aldens have been such a big help to me. I hope you will enjoy the rest of your stay. And everything will be on the house. No bill for anything, James."

"Wow!" Benny said.

"Joan, thank you very much," Mr. Alden said.

In the lobby they collided with Karen Walsh. Once again she was writing in a notebook.

"Why are you always writing in that?" Benny asked.

"Well," Karen said, "I'm checking out, so I can let you in on my secret. I write travel books. I don't like anyone to know what I'm doing, so that I can see a hotel at its best and worst. Well, *this* one is the worst. I would never recommend it."

"That's why we saw you snooping around!" Benny said.

"You saw *what*?" Karen asked.

Jessie sheepishly explained that they had followed her the afternoon before because they thought she was behind the pranks.

Mr. Alden raised his eyebrows, a bit disturbed that his grandchildren had been following people around. But before he could say anything, Karen Walsh did something unexpected. She laughed. "Yes, I guess you could call me a snoop," she said. "That's my job. I was just checking out some of the rooms, seeing how well they keep their supplies, that sort of thing."

The Aldens explained to her everything that had been going on at The Plymouth. "I think you have to give The Plymouth another chance," Grandfather said.

"Well," Ms. Walsh said, "I guess I'll have to. I'll come back in a couple of weeks and stay here again. I hope things will be better."

"I know they will be," Jessie said.

CHAPTER 11

The Mystery Man

The Aldens all stood in the lobby and Grandfather said, "This is our last day in New York. I have an appointment this afternoon. What do you children intend to do?"

"I want to swim in the purple pool," Benny said.

Henry laughed. "I'm sure by now the pool is filled with plain, *clear* water — without any purple."

"I think a swim would be very nice," Jessie said.

"I wonder why," Violet said, giggling.

Jessie blushed. "Violet, you are reading things into that."

"How can she *read* what you said when you didn't write it down?" Benny asked.

"We'll explain some other time," Henry said. "Let's go for a swim."

The Aldens went back to their rooms and changed into their suits. When they went up to the pool, Mike was sitting in his usual place. "Hi, Aldens," he said.

"Can we swim today?" Benny asked.

"Sure can," Mike replied. "Everything is in top shape."

The children went into the pool room and saw that the water was crystal clear, sparkling in the sunlight. They dived right in. "It's perfect," Violet said. "Not too hot or cold."

They swam and played and splashed for half an hour. After they had dried off, they stopped at Mike's desk.

"We're leaving tomorrow morning, so we won't see you again," Henry said.

"Well," Mike said, "I hope you had a good visit. Come back soon."

"I hope we can," Jessie said quickly. She heard Violet giggle behind her.

Back in their room, they dressed. "Let's find a hot dog stand for lunch," Benny said.

"I'm ready for that," Henry agreed. "Then what should we do?"

"I want to see the Metropolitan Museum of Art," Violet said.

"The guidebook said they have great old suits of armor there," Henry said. "Let's go."

"We mustn't forget that Grandfather is taking us to dinner and the theater tonight. We need to get back in time to dress," Jessie reminded them.

"We have to dress up?" Benny asked.

"Of course," Violet answered. "When you go to the theater in New York, you have to look nice."

They left the hotel and luckily found a hot dog vendor a block away. They bought hot dogs and cold drinks and sat down on a bench in the park to eat. When they had finished

they took a bus uptown to the museum. Together they roamed around the huge building. They looked at wonderful things: the
armor, famous paintings, Egyptian mum-
mies, a Japanese garden, and at last they all
agreed they were tired.

On the way back to the hotel, Jessie said,
"I never realized a museum could be *that*
big."

"And we didn't see a quarter of it," Violet
said. "At least according to our guidebook,
we didn't."

Grandfather was waiting for them in their
suite when they got back to the hotel. "Now,
you all have to look your best tonight for the
theater. Girls, wear your best dresses. Boys,
jackets. We'll have dinner at the restaurant
here in the hotel and then off to the theater."

"Are we going to eat in the coffee shop?"
Benny asked.

"No, this time we'll eat in the big restaurant," Grandfather answered.

The restaurant had tables with pink cloths,
candles, and flowers. The food was delicious,

and after dinner Benny said, "You know, I think I'm full."

"That's a first," said Jessie, and they all laughed.

They took a taxi to Broadway.

"Wow!" Benny said when they entered the theater. "Now I can see why we got dressed up. This is much nicer than the movie theater back in Greenfield."

"Yes, isn't it pretty?" said Violet.

The seats were dark red, and the stage was hidden by a dark-red velvet curtain. An usher took them to their seats. Soon afterwards, the lights dimmed and the orchestra played a lively overture. The Aldens could hardly wait for the curtain to go up.

And when it did, they were very surprised!

In the center of the stage was a man with silvery hair and a long, pointed nose. The mysterious man!

"That's him!" Benny whispered.

Several people around Benny said, "Ssh."

The musical was wonderful, with lots of colorful costumes and exciting dancing. But all Benny could think about was the mysterious man.

At the intermission he told Grandfather, "That was our mystery man."

Grandfather laughed. "*That* was Frederick Astor, one of Broadway's biggest stars."

"Why was he always going around the hotel in dark glasses with his coat collar pulled up around his face?" Violet asked.

"Well," Grandfather said, "often big stars don't want to be recognized and bothered by the public, so they try different disguises, as Mr. Astor obviously did."

"Now *all* the mysteries have been solved," Henry said.

The next morning as the Aldens were leaving, a woman rushed in wearing dark glasses and a hat pulled low over her face. "Is it another mystery?" Benny asked hopefully.

Just then a man ran over to the woman in

sunglasses and asked her for her autograph. The Aldens all laughed.

"Benny, I guess you are just going to have to find a mystery somewhere else," Grandfather said as they all left the hotel.

GERTRUDE CHANDLER WARNER discovered when she was teaching that many readers who like an exciting story could find no books that were both easy and fun to read. She decided to try to meet this need, and her first book, *The Boxcar Children*, quickly proved she had succeeded.

Miss Warner drew on her own experiences to write each mystery. As a child she spent hours watching trains go by on the tracks opposite her family home. She often dreamed about what it would be like to set up housekeeping in a caboose or freight car — the situation the Alden children find themselves in.

When Miss Warner received requests for more adventures involving Henry, Jessie, Violet, and Benny Alden, she began additional stories. In each, she chose a special setting and introduced unusual or eccentric characters who liked the unpredictable.

While the mystery element is central to each of Miss Warner's books, she never thought of them as strictly juvenile mysteries. She liked to stress the Aldens' independence and resourcefulness and their solid New England devotion to using up and making do. The Aldens go about most of their adventures with as little adult supervision as possible — something else that delights young readers.

Miss Warner lived in Putnam, Connecticut, until her death in 1979. During her lifetime, she received hundreds of letters from girls and boys telling her how much they liked her books.